D0771143

Our Father in heaven,
Hallowed be Your name.
Your kingdom come.
Your will be done on earth as it is in heaven.

Give us this day our daily bread.

And forgive us our debts, As we forgive our debtors.

And do not lead us into temptation,

But deliver us from the evil one.

For Yours is the kingdom and the power and the glory forever. Amen.

Matthew 6:9-13 NKJV (Read this prayer every night, and soon you will know it by heart!)

I Can Talk with God

Written and illustrated by

Debby Anderson

CROSSWAY BOOKS • WHEATON, ILLINOIS

A DIVISION OF GOOD NEWS PUBLISHERS

Dear Grown-up Readers,

God wants to have a personal growing relationship with us. As you read this book and the biblical texts (references given), pray that you and your loved ones will develop the habit of carrying on a constant conversation with our Savior—consciously living each moment with an awareness of the Lord's presence in our lives.

Prayerfully,

Debby Anderson

Gratefully acknowledging,
Dr. Elton Stetson, Ed.D., Professor of Education at Texas A&M-Commerce.

I Can Talk with God

Text and illustrations copyright © 2003 by Debby Anderson
Published by Crossway Books
      a division of Good News Publishers
      1300 Crescent Street
      Wheaton, Illinois 60187 USA

First printing 2003. Printed in Italy.

Scripture references marked NLT are taken from the *Holy Bible, New Living Translation,* copyright © 1996. Used by permission of Tyndale House Publishers, Inc., Wheaton, Ill., 60189. All rights reserved.

Scripture references marked NKJV are taken from the *New King James Version.* Copyright © 1982, Thomas Nelson, Inc. Used by permission.

Library of Congress Cataloging-in-Publication Data
Anderson, Debby.
   I can talk with God / written and illustrated by Debby Anderson.
     p. cm.
   Summary: Explains that prayer is talking with God and we can do it anywhere or anytime.
   ISBN 1-58134-416-3 (HC : alk. paper)
   1. Prayer—Christianity—Juvenile literature. [1. Prayer.] I. Title.
BV212.A53 2003
248.3'2—dc21
                         2002154405

PBI		14	13	12	11	10	09	08	07	06	05	04	03
15	14	13	12	11	10	9	8	7	6	5	4	3	2	1

To our church families
at Eastgate, Emmanuel,
and Mesquite,
who have kept our
family in their prayers
throughout our
twenty-three years as
missionaries.

And for all my readers,
I pray that your roots
may "go down deep
into the soil of God's
marvelous love."

Ephesians 3:17 NLT

...monkeys to chatter ...

God made...

...flamingoes to flute ...

. . . bees to buzz . . .

. . . tigers to roar . . .

. . . and people to talk!

He especially made people to talk
. . . so they could talk to Him!

Talking with God is called prayer. We often pray and talk with God by our beds or in church or before we eat. *1 Thessalonians 5:17*

But God wants us to talk with Him everywhere!

We can talk with God in the pumpkin patch!
We can talk with God when we hold very still
or when we move very fast! "Thank You, God,
for pumpkins, apples, and falling leaves!"

1 Thessalonians 5:18

I can talk with God at the playground—with my eyes open or closed! I can talk with God about the bad things I do because He promises to forgive! "God, I'm sorry I called my friend a mean name. Please help me to say kind words."

1 John 1:9

I can talk with God at the fire station! Whenever I hear a siren, I pray, "Dear God, please keep the fire fighters and police officers safe." The traffic light even reminds me of how God answers our prayers. Sometimes He answers "Yes" like a

green light for go. Sometimes He answers "No" like a red light for stop. But most often He answers "Wait" like a yellow light for slow. So when you ask God for something, He might say, "Yes," "No," or "Wait."

Psalm 27:14

God likes us to talk with Him. He wants to be our very best friend. He also wants to be our Savior. The most important prayer we can ever pray is to ask Jesus to rescue us from all our sin and badness. Have you done that? If not, maybe this is the time. Here is a prayer to help you know what to say:

Dear Lord Jesus,

Thank You for dying on the cross for my sin. Thank You for coming back to life again. Please forgive me and forever be my Savior, my Helper, and my Friend. Amen. *Acts 16:31*

God can talk to us, too! One of the most important ways He talks to us is in His book, the Bible. That is why we read it every day. "God, I like to read my Bible up in my tree house!"

Psalm 119:105

The Bible says that God wants us to pray for others . . .

. . . our country and leaders . . .

. . . neighbors and new babies . . .

. . . grandpas and grandmas . . .

. . . Dad's car motor . . .

. . . a friend's fever . . .

...and even for missionary children as they make new friends.

There are zillions of things to pray for, and God promises to hear every word and to help us every time! *Ephesians 6:18; Psalm 4:3*

God also wants us to pray about our own troubles and worries and about our adventures and surprises . . . .

. . . like finding a seashell . . .

losing a game . . .

. . . winning a race . . .

doing chores . . .

. . . taking spelling tests

God is so wonderful, and everything He does and makes is wonderful. God wants us to tell Him so . . . right out loud or

just quietly in our thoughts. We can even tell Him at the zoo!
"Jesus, I really like the animals You made . . . especially the giraffes!"

Psalm 126:3

Maybe someday I will talk with God while I pet a panda in China . . . or a koala in Australia!

Maybe someday I will talk with God while I go fishing in Nigeria . . .

. . . or exploring in Mexico!

Maybe someday I will talk
with God while I play
with penguins on ice . . .

. . . or eat pickles in Paris!

Maybe someday I will talk with God while I march on the moon!

But right now I can talk with God right here! "Thank You, God, that I can talk with You everywhere!"

"Don't worry about anything;
instead, pray about everything.
Tell God what you need, and
thank him for all he has done."

Philippians 4:6 NLT

Our Father in heaven,

Hallowed be Your name.

Your kingdom come.

Your will be done on earth as it is in heaven.

Give us this day our daily bread.

And forgive us our debts, As we forgive our debtors.

And do not lead us into temptation,

But deliver us from the evil one.

For Yours is the kingdom and the

power and the glory forever. Amen.

 Matthew 6:9-13 NKJV (Read this prayer every night, and soon you will know it by heart!)